Rainbows

Rainbows

A Children's Book on Unity of All People

Cheryl Green

XULON PRESS

Xulon Press
2301 Lucien Way #415
Maitland, FL 32751
407.339.4217
www.xulonpress.com

Paperback ISBN-13: 978-1-6628-2894-2

Ebook ISBN-13: 978-1-6628-2895-9

Dedication

This book is dedicated to parents who desire to teach their children about the beauty in all people.

Introduction

Sometimes people are not always nice to one another. Unkind words can be said, and people can do and say mean things. But, there is still good in people if we take the time to get to know them and see them as rainbows.

What if we were all rainbows?

We would smile
with bright colors
surrounding us each day.

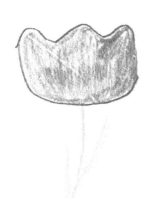

The rainiest of days
would never seem gloomy.

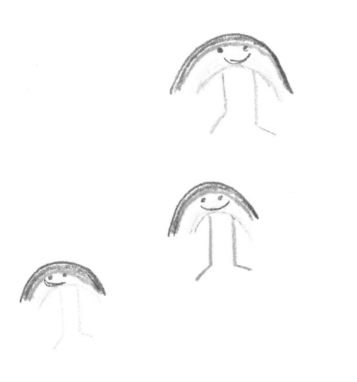

And we would all be the same----
many colors!

The sunshine would make
our colors more radiant!

There would be no more loneliness
because rainbows always have friends.

Rainbows shine brightly despite their age
because rainbows are actually ageless.

Each rainbow is different, but all shine brightly. Because after all, they are all rainbows filled with bright colors.

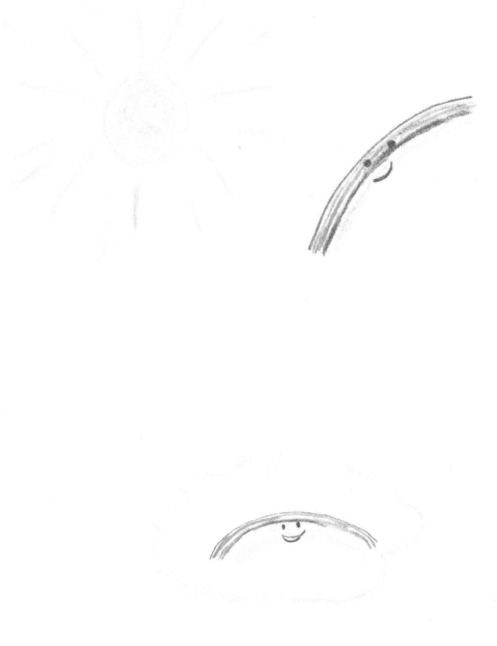

Rainbows are all priceless because their presence is special, whether they are in a puddle of water or up in the sky.

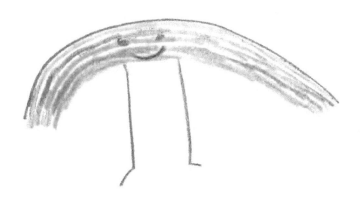

Rainbows are so happy!

They don't even argue a lot because they are too busy shining and giving off bright light.

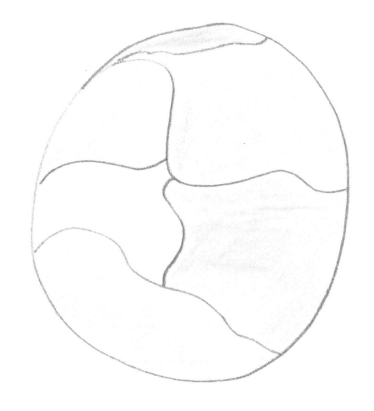

A world of rainbows is a happy world!

CPSIA information can be obtained
at www.ICGtesting.com
Printed in the USA
LVHW022143220921
698455LV00008B/343